MONA the VAMPIRE

The Big Brown Burger Monster

Hiawyn Oram

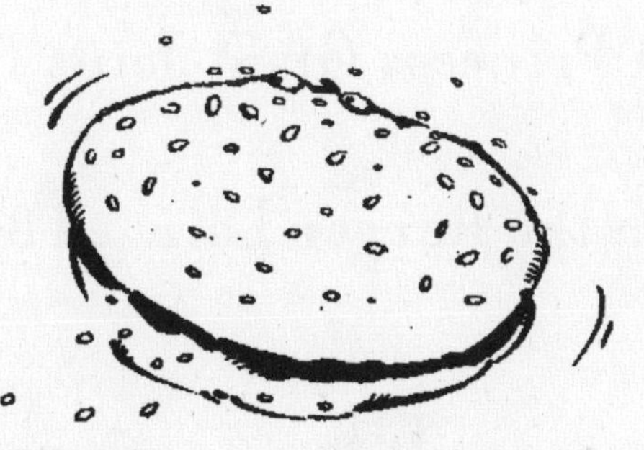

Illustrated by
Sonia Holleyman

Scholastic Canada Ltd.
Toronto New York London Auckland Sydney
Mexico City New Delhi Hong Kong

CONTENTS

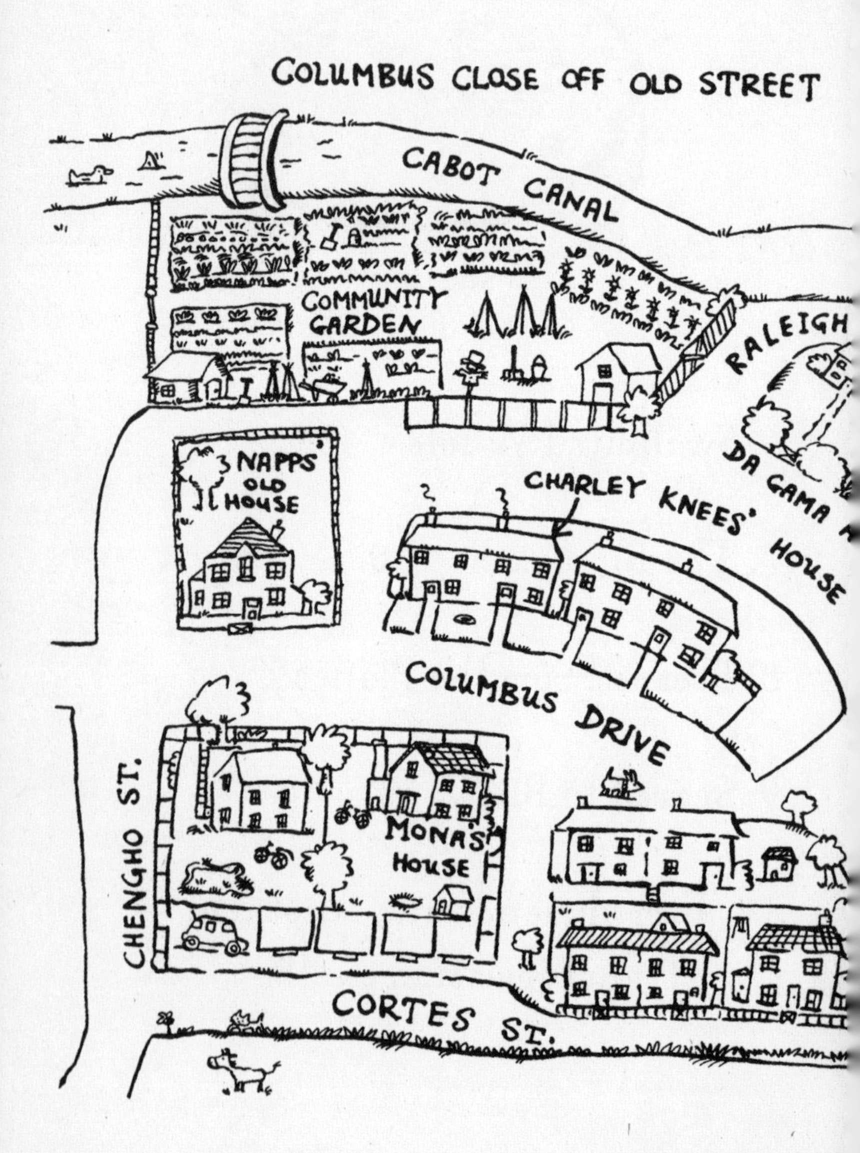
COLUMBUS CLOSE OFF OLD STREET
CABOT CANAL
COMMUNITY GARDEN
RALEIGH
NAPPS' OLD HOUSE
CHARLEY KNEES' HOUSE
DA GAMA
COLUMBUS DRIVE
MONA'S HOUSE
CHENGHO ST.
CORTES ST.

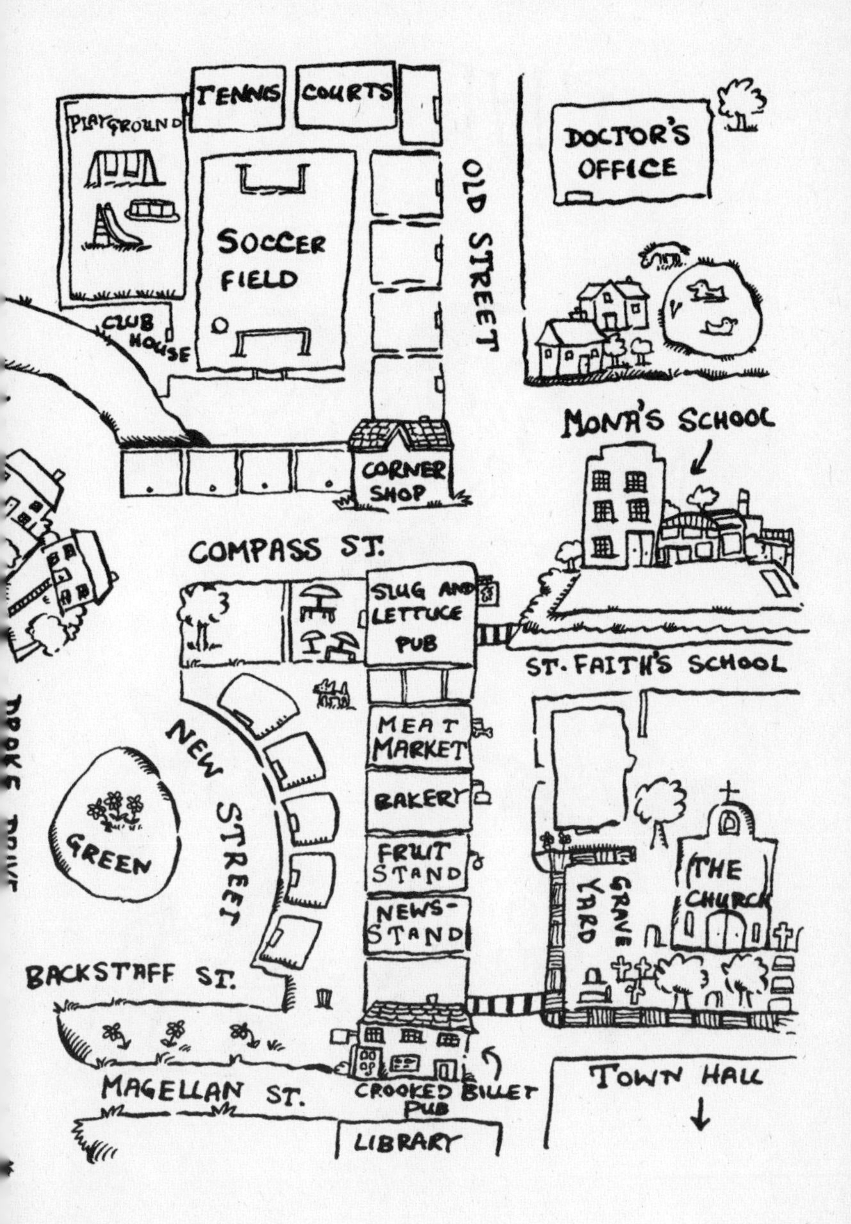

PLAYGROUND
TENNIS COURTS
SOCCER FIELD
CLUB HOUSE
OLD STREET
DOCTOR'S OFFICE
MONA'S SCHOOL
CORNER SHOP
COMPASS ST.
SLUG AND LETTUCE PUB
ST. FAITH'S SCHOOL
NEW STREET
GREEN
MEAT MARKET
BAKERY
FRUIT STAND
NEWS-STAND
GRAVE YARD
THE CHURCH
BACKSTAFF ST.
MAGELLAN ST.
CROOKED BILLET PUB
LIBRARY
TOWN HALL

THE CAST
MONA
SPIDER
FANG
GOLDEN
LILY

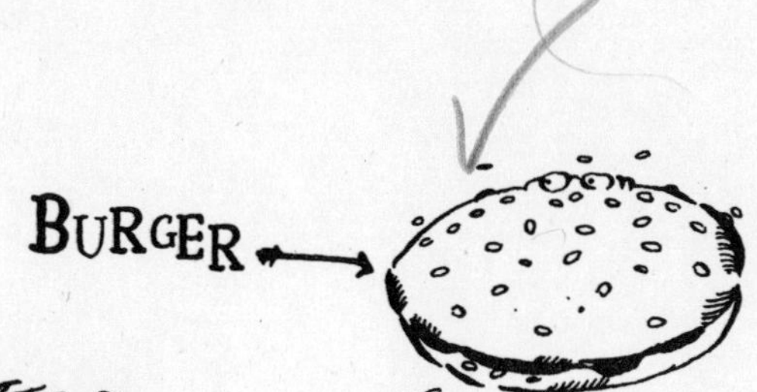
BURGER

MUM

DAD

MRS DUNCAN

Mona and Fang were in the kitchen having Tuesday dinner: burgers in big, brown whole-grain buns for Mona, and nothing for Fang if Mona's mother was watching.

Luckily, this Tuesday she wasn't watching. She was getting the dining room ready for her weekly meeting.

"Oh, and Mona," she called, "there's a little girl called Lily coming tonight. Her parents have moved in around the corner and she's your age and she'll be going to St. Faith's so I thought it'd be nice if you made friends first."

"OK," said Mona, slipping Fang another burger. "Me and Fang were just looking forward to a really nice game with someone, weren't we, Fang?"

Mmm, said Fang, his mouth too full to speak.

Mona stared around the kitchen with new interest. If there was going to be someone her age to play with, she'd better think of something someone her age would want to play.

And then, suddenly, there it was. When she half closed her eyes, the last brown burger on the counter was no longer the last burger on the counter. It had seedy eyes and huge blubbery lips and was billowing and puffing and getting bigger by the second.

"Will you look at that!" Mona leapt on to a chair.

Fang obediently arched his back.

"It's the Big Brown Burger Monster!" Mona muffled. "Don't scream, Fang, don't yell your head off with screechy scaredness . . .

Chapter 2

No Vampires Tonight

It was dark and dusty under Mona's bed. But at least it was safe from Big Brown Burger Monsters — for the moment. It was also where Mona kept her box of vampire things.

"Now," said Mona as Fang coughed and sneezed through the dust. "I suppose you're saying the only things that can scare away Burger Monsters are vampires."

Fang sneezed a definite *yes.*

"Then vampires it will have to be," said Mona, wriggling out from under the bed with the box and emptying the contents all over her bedspread. However, before she'd even stuck in her glow-in-the-dark fangs, her mother was at the door.

"Lily's here," she said.

"OK," said Mona, grabbing her dressing gown to use for a terrifying cape. "I'll be down in a minute."

"No," said her mother, removing the cape. "You'll be down now. And not as a vampire."

Mona began to explain about vampires being the only thing that could scare away Burger Monsters. But her mother wouldn't hear. "Mona," she said, in her Gentle-But-Absolutely-Firm voice. "This is my evening with my group. Mrs. Duncan hasn't been here before. Lily hasn't met you before and it's this simple: no vampires tonight."

So Mona and Fang had to go downstairs not as vampires.

"Well, don't blame me if we're gobbled," Mona warned, peering through the banister to get her first glimpse of Lily.

Chapter 3
An Unexpected Turn

Immediately, at first glimpse, her heart sank. And with each step down the stairs it sank further. Lily was clearly no Burger Scarer. Most of her was hidden behind her mother's skirt but what could be seen was trembly and delicate, her huge eyes brimming with fright.

Mrs. Duncan pried Lily's fingers from her skirt as Mona's mother did the introductions.

"She's very shy," Mrs. Duncan apologized. Mona's mother clucked sympathetically, opening the living room door.

"Well, I tell you what. Why don't they go in here? My husband's in here. He'll keep an eye on them and they can play Snap or something till we're finished."

So, under her father's watchful eye from behind his newspaper, Mona got out Snap, Tiddlywinks and the Junior Monopoly — doing her very best not to show she'd rather be upstairs preparing to meet the Burger Monster.

"OK, which one?" said Mona.

She patiently named each game.

Lily shook her head at each.

Mona offered headstands in the corner armchair.

Lily shook her head.

Mona offered TV or one of her mother's Polish-Up-Your-Karate videos.

Lily shook her head.

Mona's father offered Blind Man's Bluff, I Spy With My Little Eye, and Poker as a joke.

Lily shook her head.

Fang offered himself for stroking.

But still Lily shook her head.

Mona sighed inwardly, realizing that unless she was very careful, she and Fang were doomed to an evening of nothing. She looked over to check but her father had retired behind his newspaper. And then she made one last, desperate try.

"OK," she whispered, "do you want to come upstairs and see my vampire things . . .?"

For a second everything in the room, even breathing, froze. Then, to Mona and Fang's amazement, Lily raised her huge blue eyes and ever so slightly nodded.

Chapter 4
A Princess Giant Joins In

Lily stared but said nothing while Mona and Fang put on their vampire things, the better to show them to her.

But when Mona explained that she didn't have any more vampire things for Lily to put on, and Burger Monsters could only be scared away by vampires, she did speak — and not that faintly either . . .

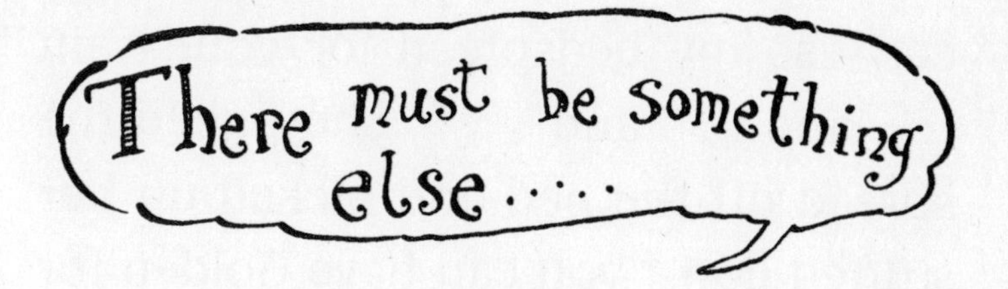

"Fang says giants," said Mona, crayoning in her vampire eyes.

"Giants?" said Lily, nervous again.

Big, big giants, coughed Fang.

"No, no," said Mona. "Not big giants. Just ordinary giants."

Immediately Lily brightened.

"I could be a Princess Giant. In your mother's high heels," she ventured.

Mona leapt up. "OK, wait here," she said and ran to her mother's room and back before Lily could change her mind.

"My mother's a karate expert so she doesn't have high heels," she panted.

"But I brought you low high heels and necklaces and lipstick and you can use my bedspread for your train . . . and . . . and . . ." she pulled the spread off the bed and picked up her stuffed lion, "you can have Golden for your faithful servant . . ."

"All right," said Lily, letting Mona and Fang help turn her into a Princess Giant in not much more than the blink of an eye. Then, with Mona announcing them the famous Most Frightening Burger Scarers, they slithered down the stairs and across the hall on their tummies so the

Burger Monster wouldn't hear them coming.

And just when it was least expecting it, they jumped up and burst into its lair, yelling . . .

Chapter 5
In the Burger Lair

"Meat-freeze, you mean. Burgers don't have any blood left in them." Mona's father was sitting in the Burger Lair, eating a cheeseburger, unaware of the danger he was in.

"Well, this one does!" cried Mona. "And you'd better watch out because it's right behind you. On the fridge, full of gnashing teeth, and the size of a flying saucer!"

"Oh no, oh help, oh where?" Mona's father ducked down in terror.

"You can't see it because you're grown up, but don't worry, it's there, isn't it Lily?" Lily nodded, her huge eyes seeing it as large as life.

"Then I'd better get out of here before it gobbles me invisibly!" said Mona's father, grabbing his burger and dashing for the Lair door. "Just make sure you take care of Her Royal Highness, the Princess Lily!"

As soon as her father had disappeared, Mona drew the curtains so her glow-in-the-dark fangs would glow better.

She lifted up her arms so her cape and her elasticized spiders would cast terrifying shadows on the walls.

Then, paling noticeably, she rummaged in a drawer for some wooden spoons and dove under the table.

"Quick, everyone! Get into the cave! It isn't dark enough. The Burger Monster isn't scared. It isn't scared at all. It's just whirr-blobbing towards us. It's smacking its two-slice lips. It's gnashing its greasy teeth. Here, Princess Giant, here, Vampire Cat, take these magic swords and swash them round or . . . PREPARE TO BE EATEN ALIVE!"

Chapter 6

Swallowed Whole

"Are we eaten yet?" breathed Lily.

"Not yet!" cried Mona. "So keep on swashing and swashing."

The three of them swashed wildly from the safety of the cave. But it was no good.

"Oh no!" cried Mona. "It isn't bothered by swords. Look, it's eaten Fang's. And now it's eating mine!"

"What'll we do?" whispered Lily.

"Don't worry, you've still got yours," said Mona. "And your magic necklaces. Use your magic necklaces to turn your sword into a magic wand. Then with your magic wand turn Golden into a Magic Genie."

"Now ask Golden to save us," said Mona. "Say, 'Golden Genie, Golden Genie, faithful Golden Genie, turn the Big Brown Burger Monster into a mouse so Fang can pounce!'" Lily hesitated.

"Go on," Mona yelled. "Hurry!"

Still Lily hesitated. *You do it!* 'hissed Fang.

Mona grabbed Golden and crawled to the mouth of the cave. But when she crawled back, she had only bad news.

"The Burger Monster wasn't afraid of Golden either. It just went, 'Yummy, yummy, a lovely fat Golden Genie' and gobbled him up. And now it's whirr-blobbing right into our cave, going,

"Yummy, yummy, a lovely fat Vampire Cat and a lovely fat Princess Giant. It's swallowing you, Fang. It's swallowing you, Lily. And now, oh whoops, oh dear, oh help, oh help . . . IT'S EVEN SWALLOWED . . . ME!"

"OK in there?" Mona's father put his head round the Burger Lair door.

"Fine!" said Mona. "The Burger Monster's swallowed us. That's all."

Whole, mewed Fang.

"Like Jonah in the whale," said Mona's father.

"Like three Jonahs in a Burger," said Mona.

"Four with Golden," said Lily, clasping Golden tightly.

"Well, you'll have to dance on its ribs for forty days and forty nights till it can't bear any more and spits you out," said Mona's father.

"Oh yes!" breathed Lily.

"Not yet!" snapped Mona, wriggling out from under the table and whirling round in circles. "Because don't you know, right now, the Burger Monster's whirr-whizzing us through space. And we don't want to be spitted out in the middle of space, do we?"

"Not without oxygen masks," said Mona's father. "Well, I'll be in the Living Room Galaxy if you need me. And good luck!"

"Come on, you two!" Mona was whirling round so hard she was already giddy. "The Burger Monster's whirr-spinning us into the Hall Galaxy . . ."

Fang and Lily scrambled to join Mona in the dark, nearly empty beauty of the Hall Galaxy.

"And now it's making for the Living Room Galaxy!" cried Mona. "It's in the Living Room Galaxy! And it's going so fast it's nearly crashing . . ."

Chapter 7
The Big Crash

"Into my meteor . . ." said a booming voice . . .

The Sofa-shaped meteor, home of me, the Lonely Meteor Giant

"Well, don't worry, we're not stopping, Meteor Giant. We're on our way . . . to the Garden Galaxy!" cried Mona.

"This is my favourite," breathed Lily as they whirled around in the starry darkness.

Me too, hissed Fang.

"No, no!" cried Mona. "Don't you know anything? This is the most dangerous galaxy. It's full of Black Holes. If we're not careful, the Burger Monster will be sucked into a black hole with us inside it . . . and that'll be the end of everything . . . we'll never get out . . ."

"Then we'll have to turn back," shivered Lily, suddenly seeing Black Holes everywhere.

So they all rattled and yelled until they had the Burger Monster whirr-whizzing back through the Living Room Galaxy into the safety of the Hall Galaxy.

Only by that time they were so giddy from spinning and whirling, they were completely out of control and could not stop.

And the next thing any of them knew, they'd whirr-whizzed where they shouldn't — and crash-landed in a terrible screeching jangle and tangle of arms and legs — right in the middle of Mona's mother's meeting.

Chapter 8

Escape from the Planet Zogg

Now we're in for it, spluttered Fang.

Six pairs of eyes stared down at them. Four pairs of eyes looked very disturbed. One pair looked very, very cross. One pair rolled in shock.

"Mona!" said the cross eyes (Mona's mother's). "What do you think you're doing?" But before Mona could even start to answer, something completely unexpected happened. Lily stood up without a tremble or a blush — and picked up Golden. She straightened her train calmly and put on a missing low high heel.

Then she spoke — or rather she erupted in a flow of words — as if she'd been holding back all her life and didn't need to hold back anymore.

“We are the famous Monster Burger Scarers . . . at your service.” She bowed low. “I am Lily the Princess Giant. This is Golden, my faithful Magic Genie. This is Mona the Vampire, Chief Scarer of Monsters and Other Things That Go Bump in the Night, and this is Fang, her assistant.”

The pair of shocked, rolling eyes — Lily’s mother’s — looked as if they were going to roll right out of her head.

But this didn't stop Lily.

"We were swallowed by the Big Brown Burger Monster, like Jonah, and whirred through many galaxies," she continued as easily as Fang might purr. "But now we're spitted out here . . . on . . ." she stifled a giggle, ". . . the great Planet Zogg."

She bowed low again but mainly because she was doubled up with giggles.

When the fit passed she pointed over to Mona's bike propped up in a corner. "And, oh look, a space capsule awaits us. If you, the great Zoggians, will allow the Chief Burger Scarer to get to it, we'll be gone in a flash and trouble you no more . . ."

Mona, her mouth open, looked over at her mother. Her mother, with her mouth open, gave a small nod and

Mona ran over to the bike. She jumped on, circled the table at great speed to show off her space-bike capsule skills, stopped to pick up the others — and fled.

Chapter 9

Scared To Bits

Mona was pedalling so hard that, once back in the hall, they almost had a very nasty crash. Luckily her father was there to catch the bike and steady them.

"Hmmm," he said. "I expect your mother's very cross — having her meeting interrupted."

"Well, she was," said Mona, dismounting. "But then Lily explained."

"Lily explained?" said Mona's father.

"Even so," said her father, "if I were you, I'd end this adventure now."

"Oh, but we can't," cried Lily, jumping up and down. "Because the Burger Monster spitted us out but it's not gone yet."

"You're right!" cried Mona, running to check the kitchen. "It's back on the fridge puffing and gnashing its teeth."

Well, when ARE you going to get rid of it? hissed Fang. *'Cause I'm famished.*

"What about Burger Bait?" said Lily. "We could lure it back into the burger box with bait and then throw it in the garbage!"

Brilliant, said Fang. *Cheese would do it.*

"Brilliant," said Mona's father, retiring to the sitting room. "And then that must be that."

"Not brilliant one bit!" said Mona, wanting Lily to join in properly but not wanting her to have all the good ideas. "It might burst out and eat the garbage men. But we could lure it into the hall here and scare it to bits. And I know how!"

She raced upstairs to the bathroom, reappearing a few moments later with her big, yellow, foot-shaped sponge, dripping and squelching wet.

Then she ran down the stairs and switched off the overhead light, leaving on the table lamps. And this time when she raised her arms, her

cape made such terrifying shadows and her spiders jiggled so horrifyingly she knew nothing would go wrong now.

"See, here it comes. Out of the kitchen, whirr-blobbing over to the bait . . ." Mona called through bared fangs. "And this time it IS frightened enough!"

Then DO it, hissed Fang from under the coat stand.

"WE ARE!" cried Mona. "WE ARE! AND NOW IT'S SO FRIGHTENED IT'S GOING TO EXPLODE. IN FACT IT IS EXPLODING! INTO A MILLION BITS. A MILLION TRILLION BITS. IT'S EXPLODING INTO SO MANY BITS. IT'S EXPLODING INTO AIR! THERE! BANG! IT'S EXPLODED!"

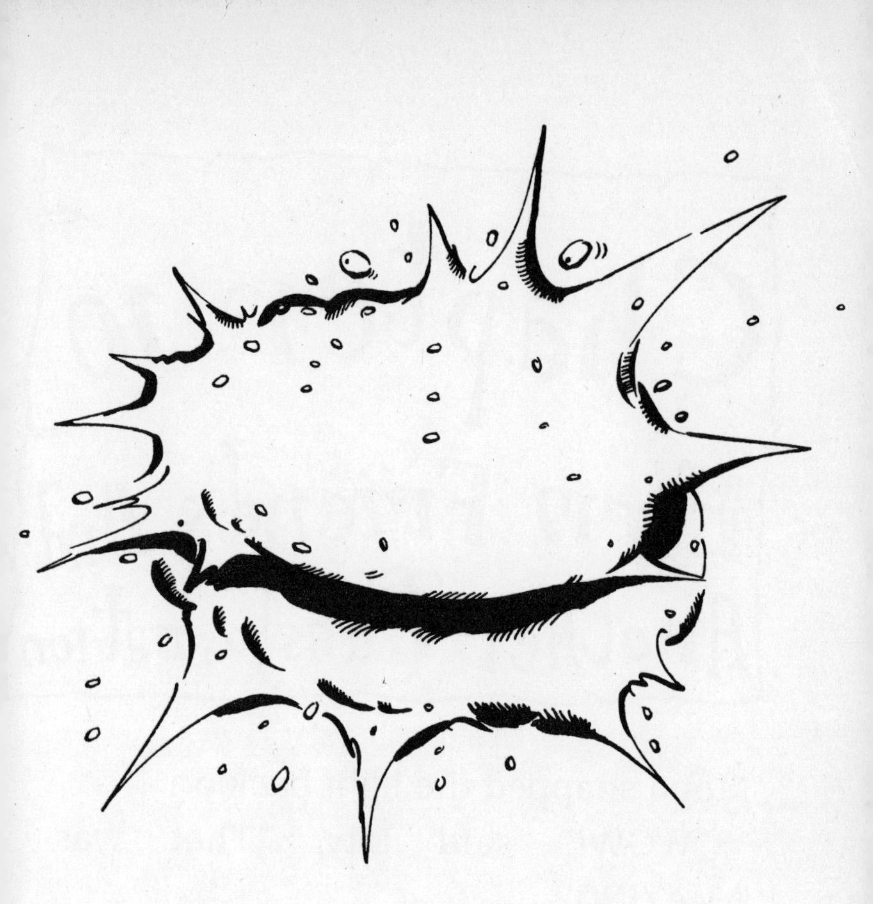

Chapter 10

Firm Friends And Another Transformation

Mona snapped the light back on.

"WOW!" said Lily, "That was AMAZING!"

Can we get something to eat now? mewed Fang.

"OK," said Mona. "Peanut butter cookies, since they're your favourite!" But before they could get to the kitchen, Mona's mother and Mrs.

Duncan emerged from the dining room.

"Mona, Lily has to go home now."

"I'm afraid we do," said Mrs. Duncan.

"Ohhhhh," Lily groaned. "Just a bit longer. I'm having the best time ever."

"Sorry," said Mrs. Duncan, taking off Lily's train. "But I must say what's happened here tonight is incredible. Why, Lily is . . . well, she's completely transformed!"

"Does that mean she can come and play tomorrow?" said Mona. "Because after Angela she can be my best friend now. And she can borrow Golden if she likes."

"Well, that's very kind and we'll see about tomorrow . . . ." Mrs. Duncan sounded a bit flustered. But she did kiss Mona's mother — which seemed like a good sign — before ushering Lily, clasping Golden, down the garden path.

And while Mona's mother said goodbye to the other members of her group, Mona and Fang went to check out a few things with her father.

"What exactly does transformed mean?" she said, taking out her fangs and cuddling up.

"Changed from one thing to another," said her father. "Usually to something better."

"Then Mum won't be cross that Lily got transformed in our house?"

"She should be very pleased," said Mona's father. "And very proud of you, as you helped it come about."

"Well, it was our game that did it," said Mona. "You see, Dad, it was only a game. There wasn't really a Burger Monster."

Not an actual one, purred Fang.

"Oh yes," said her father. "In that case, would you mind telling me where all the peanut butter cookies have gone?"

Prob'ly just transformed, yawned Fang.

And Mona didn't argue. She'd already entered the Dream Galaxy and didn't even hear the question.